For Helen with love

DIAL BOOKS FOR YOUNG READERS · A division of Penguin Young Readers Group · Published by The Penguin Group · Penguin Group (USA) Inc., 375 Hudson Street, New York, NY 10014, U.S.A. · Penguin Group (Canada), 90 Eglinton Avenue East, Suite 700, Toronto, Ontario, Canada M4P 2Y3 (a division of Pearson Penguin Canada Inc.) · Penguin Books Ltd, 80 Strand, London WC2R 0RL, England · Penguin Ireland, 25 St. Stephen's Green, Dublin 2, Ireland (a division of Penguin Books Ltd) · Penguin Group (Australia), 250 Camberwell Road, Camberwell, Victoria 3124, Australia (a division of Pearson Australia Group Pty Ltd) · Penguin Books India Pvt Ltd, 11 Community Centre, Panchsheel Park, New Delhi - 110 017, India · Penguin Group (NZ), 67 Apollo Drive, Rosedale, North Shore 0632, New Zealand (a division of Pearson New Zealand Ltd) · Penguin Books (South Africa) (Pty) Ltd, 24 Sturdee Avenue, Rosebank, Johannesburg 2196, South Africa · Penguin Books Ltd, Registered Offices: 80 Strand, London WC2R 0RL, England

Library of Congress Cataloging-in-Publication Data · Kellogg, Steven. · The Pied Piper's magic / Steven Kellogg. · p. cm.
Summary: In a story loosely based on The Pied Piper of Hamelin, an elf acquires from a miserable witch a magic pipe that allows him to transform things, including the mean-spirited Grand Duke who rules over a rat-infested town.
ISBN 978-0-8037-2818-9 · [1. Fairy tales. 2. Magic—Fiction. 3. Rats—Fiction.] I. Pied Piper of Hamelin. II. Title. · PZ8.K366Pi 2009
[E]-dc22   2008012267

The full-color artwork was prepared using ink and pencil line, watercolor washes, and acrylic paints.

the Pied Piper's Magic

STEVEN KELLOGG

Dial Books for Young Readers

One day long ago and far away, a small elf in search of
work came upon a tumbledown house. The elf was so poor
that his clothes were made of rags and patches. But he was a
good-natured fellow, and when he spotted a woman slumped
on the porch, he approached her with a hopeful smile.

"I'm Peterkin," he said. "With your permission I could spend a few hours making myself useful around your cottage. Perhaps you might be willing to pay me a penny or two?"

"I'm Elbavol," grumbled the woman. "I'm a retired witch who was a worthless witch even back in the days when I was a working witch. I haven't a penny to pay you for anything. Be gone!"

Peterkin had never met such a dreary person, and he decided to try to cheer her up.

"Never mind the penny," he said. "I'll just spend a few minutes tidying the place, and then I'll be on my way."

The elf worked so quickly that he seemed to be everywhere at once, and he didn't quit until the cottage glowed from the cellar to the chimney.

For a moment Elbavol almost smiled. "Little elf," she said, "I am grateful for your kindness. Although I haven't a penny to pay you, let me give you this pipe. I was told long ago that it has a magical power, but I have never discovered what that power is. Perhaps you can."

"Oh thank you, Elbavol," cried Peterkin. But to his dismay the woman's dark mood returned.

"Leave me to my solitude," she muttered. "I am lonely, old, and worn out. Go away!"

The pied elf set out again to look for work, but Eldavor's gloom followed him. He studied the pipe and said, "I wish your magic could have made that sad lady smile."

To cheer himself up he tried to play a few notes, but to his surprise the pipe made the sounds of *letters*!

Even better, when he played *B-U-T-T-E-R-F-L-I-E-S* or *B-E-E-S*
or *B-L-U-E-B-I-R-D-S* those creatures mysteriously appeared.
Next he tried *D-E-E-R*.

"Amazing!" cried the elf.

He was so excited that he flipped over backward. The pipe responded by reversing the letters and singing *R-E-E-D*. The deer was instantly transformed into a reed.

Peterkin experimented by flipping once again. The pipe sang *D-E-E-R,* and sure enough, the reed turned back into a deer.

Filled with wonder Peterkin exclaimed, "From now on, enchanted pipe, you shall be my traveling companion and my friend!"

He happily resumed his journey, so caught up in his pipe-playing that he forgot all about dreary Elbavol.

Many miles later the forest pathway joined a winding road that led the elf to the gates of a dark city. Clouds of foul-smelling smoke belched from the chimneys and hovered menacingly over the rooftops.

As Peterkin entered the gates he was amazed to see thousands and thousands of rats. They scuttled everywhere, ignoring the children who were trying to shoo them away.

"Where are your parents?" Peterkin asked the children.

"The Grand Duke has ordered them to work all day
and all night in his factories," replied the children sadly.
"He rules the city and everyone fears him."

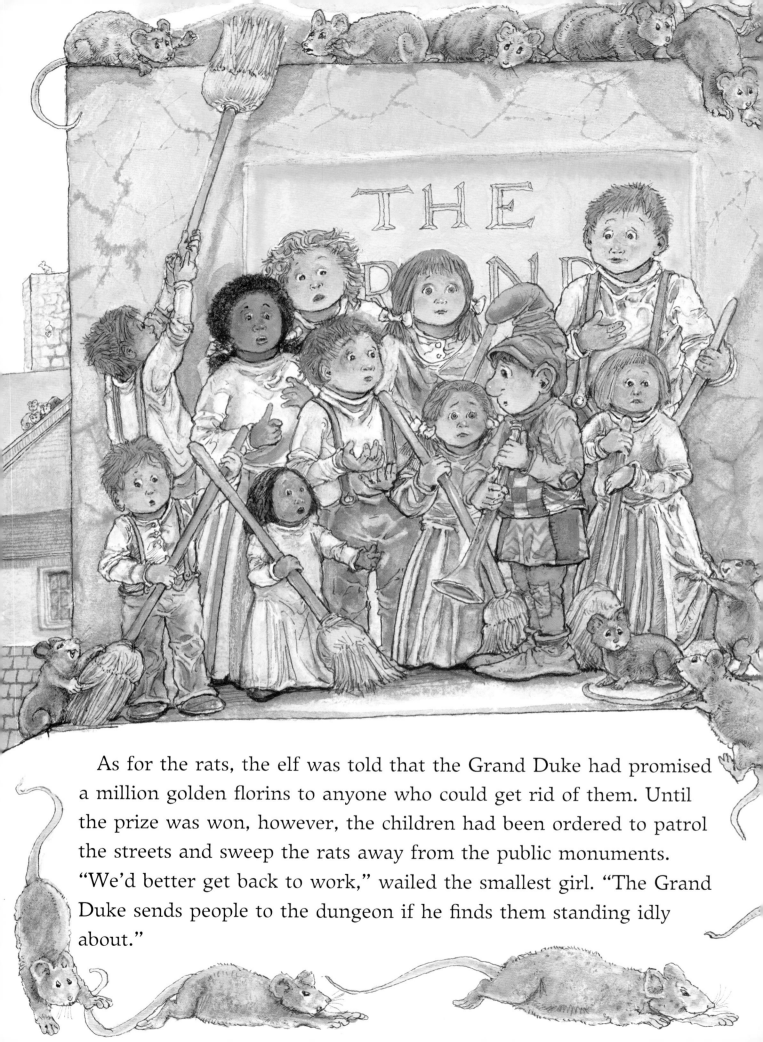

As for the rats, the elf was told that the Grand Duke had promised a million golden florins to anyone who could get rid of them. Until the prize was won, however, the children had been ordered to patrol the streets and sweep the rats away from the public monuments. "We'd better get back to work," wailed the smallest girl. "The Grand Duke sends people to the dungeon if he finds them standing idly about."

"I will earn that reward!" cried Peterkin. "And then I will give it to you and your parents so you can leave this gloomy city and live happily together as parents and children should!"

He lifted his pipe and played, *R-A-T-S! R-A-T-S! R-A-T-S!*

Instantly rats began pouring from cellars, windows, and rooftops.

As growing herds of rats swarmed into line behind Peterkin, the excited children forgot that they had been forbidden by the Grand Duke to interrupt their parents' work, and they burst into the factories.

"Come quickly!" they shouted. "A pied piper is rounding up the rats, and he has promised to give us the reward!"

By nightfall every rat in the city had been led to the Grand Duke's palace.

Remembering the deer and the reed, the elf played *R-A-T-S! R-A-T-S! R-A-T-S!* Then he flipped over backward.

S-T-A-R! S-T-A-R! S-T-A-R! sang the pipe. The crowd gasped,
then cheered, as the rats became shimmering stars.

The cheering aroused the Grand Duke.

"SILENCE!" he roared. "Return to the factories at once!"

"Wait!" cried the children. "It's a celebration. The rats are gone, and the piper has earned the reward!"

"Ha!" scoffed the Grand Duke. "For inciting a riot and disrupting my sleep, the piper's reward shall be fifty years in the dungeon!"

"You are even more miserable than Elbavol," cried Peterkin.

"Elbavol? Who is Elbavol?" bellowed the Grand Duke.

Suddenly the pied piper was struck by an idea.

Peterkin played a single word, strong and clear: *S-T-A-R!*
He followed it with his highest backward flip yet.

R-A-T-S! sang the pipe. Overhead one especially large
and sparkly star exploded, and a shower of chattering rats
plummeted onto the balcony, flattening the Grand Duke.

Peterkin played *R-A-T-S*, and the animals leaped to obey,
dragging the shrieking Grand Duke behind them.

The parents and children followed as the rest of the stars swooped down to light their way through the city gates, into the forest, and finally to Elbavol's cottage.

"Elbavol, wake up!" called Peterkin. "I have discovered the secret of the pipe's magic!"

He played *E-L-B-A-V-O-L! E-L-B-A-V-O-L! E-L-B-A-V-O-L!* And
with a triumphant laugh he flipped over backward.
L-O-V-A-B-L-E! L-O-V-A-B-L-E! L-O-V-A-B-L-E! sang the pipe.

Elbavol stared at the elf in amazement. "Lovable?" she asked.
"Yes. Truly lovable!" said Peterkin.
And for the first time in her life, the woman smiled.

The glow of that smile surrounded the entire group,
including the Grand Duke. The rats faded away as he
gazed in wonder at Elbavol.

Then, for the first time in *his* life, the Grand Duke smiled back. "Lovable," he whispered.

Suddenly he and Elbavol, finding both themselves and each other lovable, were transformed. Their loneliness and unhappiness disappeared, and they fell joyfully into each other's arms.

"I have no wish to return to the palace," said the Grand Duke. "Wise and noble piper, please accept this key to the city as the reward for your heroic deeds."

But the pied piper presented the key to the parents.

He asked them to transform the city into a lovable place where they and their children could live together happily.

Elbavol and the Grand Duke were married, and after the wedding feast, Peterkin resumed his journey, eager to discover new uses for his magic pipe.

A year later he returned to the city. Some of the children spotted him making his way across the valley, and with cries of joy they ran to welcome him.

It warmed Peterkin's heart to see that the buildings now
glowed from the cellars to the chimneys, and that the streets
were filled with laughter and sunlight and music.